P9-BAV-165

You're Here for a Reason

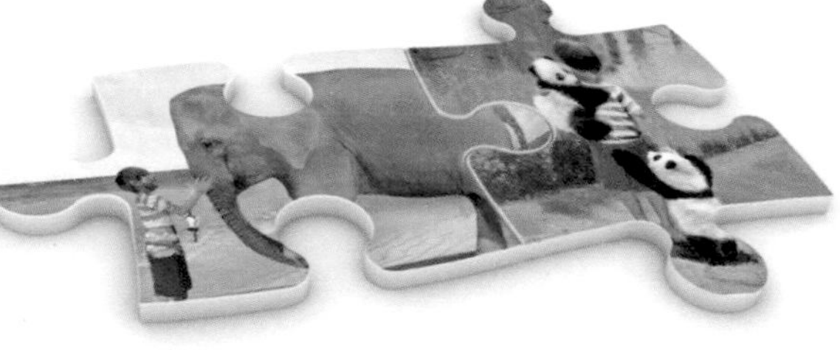

Nancy Tillman

FEIWEL AND FRIENDS
NEW YORK

You're here for a reason, you certainly are.
The world would be different without you, by far.

If not for your hands and your eyes and your feet,
the world, like a puzzle, would be incomplete.

STOP

Even the smallest of things that you do
blossom and multiply far beyond you.

A kindness, for instance, may triple for days . . .

or set things in motion in different ways.

It travels much further
than you'll ever know . . .

under the treetops . . .

over the snow . . .

till it’s wandered . . .

and fluttered . . .

and floated . . .

and twirled—

making things happen
all over the world.

You're here for a reason.
It's totally true.
You're part of a world that
is counting on you.

So don't be too worried
if some days fall flat.
Good things can happen,
even from that.

Life can be tricky, there isn't a doubt.
You'll skin your knees trying to figure it out.

But life works together, the good and the bad,
the silly and awful, and happy and sad,
to paint a big picture we can't always see . . .
a picture that needs you, most definitely.

Remember that next time a day goes all wrong . . .

to somebody else,
you will always be strong.

And that ball that you lose or that kite you let go
could make someone's day—

you just never know!

You're here for a reason. If you think you're not,
I would just say that perhaps you forgot—

a piece of the world that is precious and dear
would surely be missing if you weren't here.

If not for your smile and your laugh and your heart,
this place we call home would be minus a part.

Thank goodness you're here!
Thank goodness times two!

I just can't imagine a world without you.

To my magnificent granddaughter, Bonnie Jayne Tillman. I just can't imagine a world without you.
—N.T.

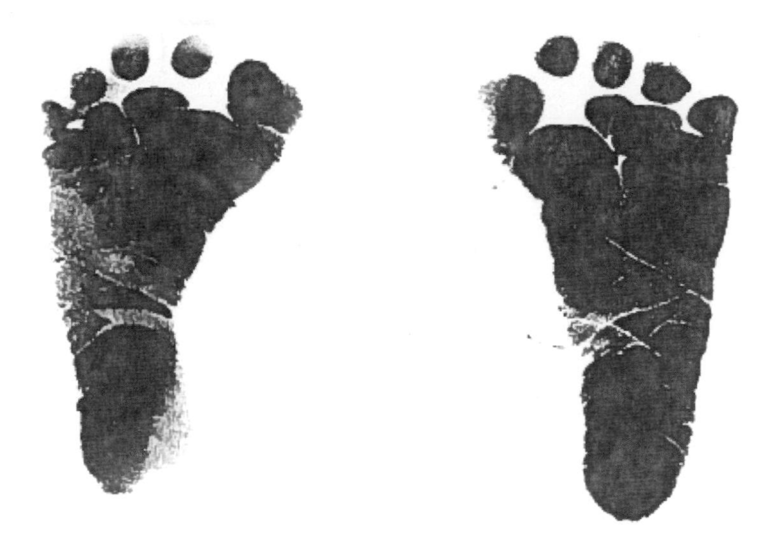

A FEIWEL AND FRIENDS BOOK
An Imprint of Macmillan

Printed in the United States of America by Phoenix Color Corp., Hagerstown, Maryland.
For information, address Feiwel and Friends, 175 Fifth Avenue, New York, N.Y. 10010.

Feiwel and Friends books may be purchased for business or promotional use. For information on bulk purchases, please contact the Macmillan Corporate and Premium Sales Department at (800) 221-7945 x5442 or by e-mail at specialmarkets@macmillan.com.

Library of Congress Cataloging-in-Publication Data Available

ISBN: 978-1-250-05626-9

Book design by Nancy Tillman and Kathleen Breitenfeld

The artwork was created digitally using a variety of software painting programs on a Wacom tablet. Layers of illustrative elements are first individually created, then merged to form a composite. At this point, texture and mixed media (primarily chalk, watercolor, and pencil) are applied to complete each illustration.

Feiwel and Friends logo designed by Filomena Tuosto

First Edition: 2015

10 9 8 7 6 5 4 3 2

mackids.com

You are loved.